SCALPED

JASON AARON
WRITER

R.M. GUÉRA
ARTIST

THE GNAWING

GIULIA BRUSCO
WITH TRISH MULVIHILL
(CHAPTER 2)
COLORISTS

STEVE WANDS
LETTERER

JOCK
ORIGINAL SERIES COVERS

MATT FRACTION
INTRODUCTION

SCALPED created by
JASON AARON and R.M. GUÉRA

KAREN BERGER
SVP - Executive Editor

WILL DENNIS
Editor - Original Series

MARK DOYLE
Associate Editor - Original Series

BOB HARRAS
Group Editor - Collected Editions

ROBBIN BROSTERMAN
Design Director - Books

DC COMICS

DIANE NELSON
President

DAN DIDIO and JIM LEE
Co-Publishers

GEOFF JOHNS
Chief Creative Officer

PATRICK CALDON
EVP-Finance and Administration

JOHN ROOD
EVP-Sales, Marketing and
Business Development

AMY GENKINS
SVP-Business and Legal Affairs

STEVE ROTTERDAM
SVP-Sales and Marketing

JOHN CUNNINGHAM
VP-Marketing

TERRI CUNNINGHAM
VP-Managing Editor

ALISON GILL
VP-Manufacturing

DAVID HYDE
VP-Publicity

SUE POHJA
VP-Book Trade Sales

ALYSSE SOLL
VP-Advertising
and Custom Publishing

BOB WAYNE
VP-Sales

MARK CHIARELLO
Art Director

Cover illustration and logo design by JOCK

SCALPED: THE GNAWING

DC Comics, 1700 Broadway, New York, NY 10019
A Warner Bros. Entertainment Company.
Printed by World Color Press, Inc., Dubuque, IA, USA
(4/21/10) First Printing.
ISBN: 978-1-4012-2717-3

SUSTAINABLE
FORESTRY
INITIATIVE

Certified Fiber Sourcing
www.sfiprogram.org

Fiber used in this product line meets the
sourcing requirements of the SFI program.
www.sfiprogram.org PWC-SFICOC-260

THE GNAWING, OR,
THE LEGEND OF THE ALABAMA CORN SNAKE

Do you know the story of the Alabama Corn Snake? I swear I'll never let it be forgotten and I'll never let those words slip too far from my tongue. I'll tell you, too, just after I tell you why I love SCALPED:

My favorite comics make me marvel over their construction. They look and feel and read like little watchworks, with points of view and perspectives so alien that the experience of engaging with them, of reading them and getting lost in their stories, feels like taking a trip somewhere in a new suit of skin. I read them again and again, and each time is a joy because at no point does the writer in me pipe up to say anything more than, "Man… how did they do that?" I have no notes, I don't see where it's coming or going; I don't think about how I would write them any differently. My favorite comics are so good I can actually read them and not just size 'em up.

I'm not sure if you realize how much that little voice ruins stuff for people like me all the time, but it happens ALL THE TIME.

So I was going to talk about SCALPED through that lens – that it's one of my favorite comics going, if not my very favorite, because, month in and month out I fall in love with the thing all over again. I've read the entire run a good half-dozen times now and reread the run every time a new collection like this comes out. What Jason Aaron and R. M. Guéra have here deepens and strengthens the longer it goes; it both remains great and becomes greater as it gains in size and sweep. I love this book. I love it, I love it, I love it.

Then I realized, well, hell – this is the sixth fucking collection. What kind of introductory expectations does anyone rightfully have for book SIX of… howevermany it'll be? If you're reading this, you are, like me, on Team SCALPED and don't need convincing to buy or read the thing. So rather than tell you what you already know – that this book beats the fucking band like it's owed money – let me maybe tell you something you DON'T know, and at least, this way, if I'm lucky, you won't feel like this is ripping you off.

And what you don't know, I am sure of in my very bones, is the legend of the Alabama Corn Snake. It's a story that mommas tell their babies and daddies ruminate over way down in Shelby County, Alabama.

Came a time when life in Shelby Co. wasn't what it is today, and guys you'd not necessarily want hanging around were in, fact, hanging around. I'm talking of course about Methodists, but you can fill that blank in with whatever undesirables you like. Down in the SC it was the Methodists, and that was what it was. It was a different time.

Gangs of Methodist toughs would cajole and threaten, would bend and break the law. They'd hiss at young mothers and cuss at grandmothers; they threw rocks at the men and chased down the boys with switches. The county was under siege until one man fought back.

And they called him the Alabama Corn Snake. I think because he'd run out of cornfields and beat the hell out of everybody then go running away again, I'm not sure of the etymology of the thing.

I do know this: Brandishing a sock-full of nickels and a long steel-handled flashlight (his "Methodist Masher," he called it), the Alabama Corn Snake took back the night, one skull fracture at a time. He made those Methodists renounce their heathen Methodist god or suffer even greater pummeling.

The Alabama Corn Snake saved my life from a wilding pack of Methodists one brutal August night as I stopped for gas, heading up I-65 from Montgomery to Huntsville where I was attending Space Camp for a record tenth time.

I stood, frozen in fear, as he mashed Methodist after Methodist, sock to flashlight and back again, spattering blood and shattering faith as easily as you or I would wipe bug guts from a windshield.

And when he was done we stared at each other, I in my sky-blue jumpsuit and he in his ROLL TIDE T-shirt and Adidas track-shorts. The Methodists coughed and wheezed and prayed for a god who would not come and I asked him, "Alabama Corn Snake! What happens when there aren't no more Methodists to punish? How on earth will you occupy this monster that lives inside of you and clearly cries out for bloodshed and vengeance?"

"It's okay," said the Alabama Corn Snake. "I'm going to write comic books."

Jason Aaron IS the Alabama Corn Snake. I know because I saw it with my own eyes. Next time you see him, say it to him. Alabama Corn Snake. And watch the devils and wolves that run wild inside the man and gnaw on his very bones come to the surface once more.

Matt Fraction
Portland, OR

Matt Fraction is an Eisner Award-winning writer whose works include THE FIVE FISTS OF SCIENCE, CASANOVA, THE INVINCIBLE IRON MAN *and* UNCANNY X-MEN.

WHO'S WHO

SPECIAL AGENT DASHIELL BAD HORSE

As a teenager, Dash left the Prairie Rose Reservation and never looked back. Years later, after stints as everything from an underground fighter to a soldier in Kosovo, circumstances—and the FBI—forced him to return on a mission to bring down the Rez's corrupt crimelord, Chief Lincoln Red Crow, by posing as Red Crow's enforcer in the local police department.

CHIEF LINCOLN RED CROW

A former protestor and radical turned powerful gangster and political figure, Red Crow is overseeing the opening of a casino he hopes to see restore glory to his people and cash to his wallet—and he'll take out anyone who stands in his way, by any means necessary.

GINA BAD HORSE

Dash's estranged mother and Red Crow's former comrade (and lover), Gina had stayed true to her activist roots, earning her many enemies both inside and outside the Rez. Involved in a shooting that left two FBI agents dead during her radical days, she had recently been desperately trying to reconnect with her prodigal son—until she herself ended up murdered.

AGENT BAYLIS NITZ

Dash's ruthless FBI supervisor has held a grudge against Red Crow and Gina ever since their involvement with the murder of two of his fellow agents decades ago. He's forced Dash to pin a murder, any murder, on his archnemesis Red Crow...and if the victim happens to be Dash himself, Nitz won't lose any sleep.

DIESEL

A white wannabe brave, Diesel claims to be 1/16th Kickapoo, and he's psychotic enough to force everyone to go along. His criminal enterprises have put him at murderous odds with Red Crow's drive to clean up whatever crime he himself can't monopolize. His secret status as FBI Special Agent Brett Fillenworth is known to Dash, but that won't stop Dash from seeking revenge over the death of a young boy Diesel gunned down—a boy Dash had taken under his wing.

CAROL ELLROY

As distant from her dad the Chief as Dash was from his mother, Carol's sexually self-destructive, and she's been pushing her illicit, torrid affair with Dash to the limit.

SHUNKA

Red Crow's right hand man and most loyal enforcer, Shunka is suspicious of Dash — and wary of his boss's sentimentality.

CATCHER

One of Red Crow and Gina's former radical running buddies, this Rhodes scholar turned hopeless alcoholic claims that his people's revered Thunder Beings have been sending him visions of impending doom—all centered on Dash.

OFFICER FRANKLIN FALLS DOWN

The only honest cop on the Rez, Officer Falls Down was assigned to investigate Gina Bad Horse's murder and he may be getting closer to the truth than anyone wants.

THE HMONGS

An Asian-American organized crime outfit with a vested interest in Red Crow's dealings, the Hmongs have offered to send in an "expert" named Mr. Brass to help ensure Red Crow's success—and Red Crow returned the favor by sending Brass to jail.

CHAPTER 1

I HAD A *DREAM* LAST NIGHT.

I WAS FALLING. AND THE WHOLE WORLD WAS FALLING WITH ME.

GINA WAS THERE. SHE WAS FALLING TOO. I TRIED TO GRAB HER HAND, BUT I COULDN'T REACH IT. SHE FELL ON PAST ME.

WHAT YOU THINK IT *MEANS?*

MEANS YOU STILL GOT A LOTTA *WORK* TO DO.

AND MAYBE NOT A LOT OF *TIME* IN WHICH TO DO IT.

THE CHEYENNE HAVE A STORY. THEY SAY THERE'S A GREAT BIG POLE SOMEWHERE, AND THIS POLE IS WHAT HOLDS UP THE EARTH.

AND THE GREAT WHITE GRANDFATHER BEAVER OF THE NORTH IS ALWAYS *GNAWING* AT THAT POLE.

HE'S BEEN GNAWING AT IT FOR A LONG, LONG TIME, AND IT'S ALREADY HALF CHEWED UP.

WHEN THE PEOPLE DO SOMETHING TO MAKE HIM ANGRY, THE OLD GRANDFATHER BEAVER GETS TO GNAWIN' FASTER.

PRETTY SOON, HE'LL HAVE GNAWED ALL THE WAY THROUGH.

AND THEN THAT POLE WILL TOPPLE AND THE WHOLE WORLD WILL CRASH INTO BOTTOMLESS NOTHING.

AND THAT WILL BE THE END OF EVERYTHING. THE END OF ALL ENDS.

YOU'RE GODDAMN RIGHT YOU WILL. WAR COMES TO RED CROW'S DOORSTEP, THEN SOONER OR LATER, HE'S GONNA PULL A TRIGGER ON SOMEONE.

AND WHEN HE DOES, YOUR FUCKING ASS BETTER BE RIGHT FUCKING THERE TO SEE IT.

AND WHAT IF *I'M* THE ONE HE'S PULLING THE FUCKING TRIGGER ON?

DON'T EVEN WORRY ABOUT THAT. HE GAVE *YOU* THE JOB OF FINDING THE AGENT, RIGHT? SO JUST DO WHAT YOU DO BEST. GO BEAT THE SHIT OUT OF SOMEONE. LOOK LIKE YOU'RE POUNDING THE PAVEMENT, SEARCHING FOR ANSWERS.

JUST BUY YOURSELF SOME TIME. WE ARE SO FUCKING CLOSE HERE. I CAN FEEL IT.

YOU CAN DO THIS, BAD HORSE. THIS IS WHAT YOU FUCKING TRAINED FOR. DON'T LET ME DOWN.

I DON'T HEAR NOTHIN' YET.

HELLO?

CHAPTER 2

I JUST WANNA *TALK* TO HIM IS ALL, GRANNY.

I CAN TELL YOU WHERE TO LOOK FOR HIM. DON'T MEAN YOU'LL FIND HIM THOUGH. HE'S A HARD MAN TO PIN DOWN, THAT ONE.

BUT *NOBODY'S* GONNA WANNA TALK TO YA ABOUT THEM OLD DAYS. THOSE WERE *BAD* TIMES. *LOTSA* FOLKS DID THINGS BACK THEN THEY AIN'T PROUD OF.

YOU AIN'T GOT *NO* RIGHT MAKIN' 'EM RELIVE ALL THAT.

SO... UH... HOW'S *DINO* MENDIN'?

LOST AN EYE, BUT THE REST OF HIM SEEMS TO BE HOLDING UP ALL RIGHT.

IT WAS *RED CROW* THAT SAVED HIM, YOU KNOW?

YEAH, I HEARD.

I DON'T KNOW WHAT TO MAKE OF THAT MAN NO MORE, I SURELY DON'T. JUST WHEN I'M READY TO GIVE UP ON HIM FOR GOOD, HE UP AND SURPRISES ME.

MAYBE I'M CRAZY BUT SOMETHING TELLS ME...

YEAH?

WHERE THE FUCK ARE YOU? THE POLICE RADIO'S FUCKING *EXPLODING* WITH CHATTER! SOMETHING JUST HAPPENED AT THE STATION! GET THE FUCK OVER THERE RIGHT FUCKING *NOW!*

I'M KINDA BUSY HERE.

I DON'T GIVE A FUCK WHAT YOU'RE DOING! GET TO THE STATION! FIND OUT WHAT THE FUCK'S GOING ON!

CALL ME AS SOON AS YOU KNOW SOMETHING!

THIS COULD BE IT, KID.

HEY, YOU, WHAT THE FUCK HAPPENED HERE?

BAW

A PRISONER WAS TRYING TO ESCAPE. HE WAS SHOT AND KILLED. EVERYONE ELSE IS FINE.

WELL THANK CHRIST FOR THAT. WHO SHOT HIM? *YOU?*

YOU WANNA READ THE REPORT, I'LL SEND YOU A COPY.

PLEASE DO.

LOTTA FUCKING *WITNESSES* AROUND. I'M SURE THEY'LL ALL BACK UP YOUR STORY THOUGH, RIGHT?

I'M SURE THEY WILL.

YEAH...

WHO YOU GOT IN THE BOX?

WHAT MAKES YOU THINK THERE'S ANYONE BACK THERE?

I DON'T KNOW, FUCKING INTUITION, I GUESS. WHY DON'T WE GO SEE?

WHATEVER THE FUCK YOU'RE TRYING TO PULL, IT WON'T WORK. I FUCKING *GOT* YOU THIS TIME, ASSHOLE.

WE GOTTA FIND THAT MOTHERFUCKER.

FIND THAT SON OF A BITCH.

GONNA BE A BUSY DAY, FESTUS. RECKON WE BETTER GET A MOVE ON.

HEH... WELL LOOKIE THERE NOW.

I GUESS PIGS *CAN* FLY.

CHAPTER 5

YOU KNOW, COME TOMORROW, EVERYBODY ON THE REZ WILL HAVE HEARD ABOUT THE *BEATING* YOU TOOK FROM JOHNNY TONGUE. HOW YOU PLAN ON EXPLAINING THAT TO PEOPLE?

THE REZ IS SAFE. IT WASN'T MADE INTO NO WARZONE. AND JOHNNY TONGUE AND HIS BOYS WILL NEVER BE HEARD FROM AGAIN.

I DON'T HAVE TO EXPLAIN A GODDAMN THING TO ANYBODY.

Jason Aaron & R. M. Guéra

End